This wasn't going to be fun.

Have we discussed ice water? Let's talk about it. I HATE ICE WATER! I hate being cold and wet in the wintertime. Hey, if Alfred wanted me to save him, he should have fallen into the creek in July. I would have been glad to dive in and give him some help.

But in the middle of December? There was no way this dog was going to...

"Hankie, help me! Help me, please!"

His voice was getting weaker, a tiny cry in a frozen world.

I took a deep breath and squared my enormous...no, my shoulders weren't enormous. They were thin, weak, and pitiful, and they felt like spaghetti. I was beyond scared, but you know what? All at once my mind was clear.

This wasn't going to be fun.

I crept out on the ice. "I'm coming, son, don't worry about a thing." My paws slipped and slid on the ice...

The Christmas
Turkey Disaster

John R. Erickson

Illustrations by Gerald L. Holmes

Maverick Books, Inc.

MAVERICK BOOKS, INC.
Published by Maverick Books, Inc.
P.O. Box 549, Perryton, TX 79070
Phone: 806.435.7611
www.hankthecowdog.com

First published in the United States of America by Maverick Books, Inc. 2015.

1 3 5 7 9 10 8 6 4 2

Copyright © John R. Erickson, 2015

LIBRARY OF CONGRESS CONTROL NUMBER: 2015913386

978-1-59188-166-7 (paperback); 978-1-59188-266-4 (hardcover)

Hank the Cowdog® is a registered trademark of John R. Erickson.

Printed in the United States of America

For Carlos Casso, the guy who records and produces the Hank audios at the Audio Refinery. Carlos, Hank, and I have rocked many a baby to sleep since 1982.

CONTENTS

CHAPTER ONE

The Bed Riot

It's me again, Hank the Cowdog. It was the end of November, as I recall. No, wait, it was the middle of December, the day before Christmas, but before we say another word about the Turkey Disaster, I want to make a statement for the record.

Ready? Pay attention.

If they don't want their dogs getting into the groceries, they should shut the car doors. It wasn't my fault.

There, now we can get on with the story—which, by the way, is going to be pretty scary. If you're not prepared for a story that will chill your liver, you'd better find something else to do, because this story is guaranteed to...

You know, I'm not sure we should go on. Maybe you think I'm kidding about this being one of the scariest stories of my whole career, but I'm not. I mean, when I saw that kid thrashing around in a frozen pond...

Tell you what, we'll go on with the story, but if it gets too heavy, you can just close the book and...I don't know, go brush your teeth or something. Nobody will say a word about it.

Okay, where were we? Oh yes, Christmas Eve day. After two weeks of nice fall weather, a blue norther had come roaring down from Canada and, fellers, it was cold, seriously cold. The temperature was down around zero, and Drover and I awoke to find ourselves covered with frost. Old Man Winter was knocking on the door, and there we were, shivering on our stinking gunny sack beds in an unheated office.

I've never been the kind of dog who craves luxury. Some dogs do, you know. They live in town, sleep inside a warm house, and curl up every night on some kind of store-bought cushion-bed with satin sheets and the smell of perfume.

I've never expected such pampering, and wouldn't want it even if it was offered, but for crying out loud! We were going into winter with the same gunny sack beds we'd been using for months. Years. They were threadbare and cold, and let's be honest: they stank. Hey, when a ranch dog notices that his bed stinks, you'd better believe that things have gotten out of control.

Sorry, I don't mean to rave, but when I woke up that morning, covered with frost crystals and inhaling stale fumes that were coming from my own bed, it started my day off on a sour note.

I raised my head and noticed the pile of frost next to me. It was still asleep, but shivering and grunting. "Drover, must you grunt in your sleep?"

"I'm not asleep."

"Well, you're grunting in your un-sleep."

"I'm c-c-cold."

"So am I, but do you hear me grunting about it?"

"Yeah, you grunted all night long. I thought I was sleeping in a hog pen."

"It wasn't me."

"Was too."

"Was not!"

"Was too, two, three, four, five, six, seven!" He raised his head and gave me a silly grin. "I got you on that one."

"Oh brother. This is so childish." I pushed myself up to a standing position and tested my frozen legs. "Let me point out that you didn't 'get'

3

me. What you said was nonsense. It wasn't an argument based on evidence. It would never stand up in a court of law and I can blow it to pieces with a thoughtful, well-reasoned reply." I leaned toward him and yelled, "Not, not, pitty-pot, give a dog a bone! There, I rest my case. I was *not* grunting in my sleep."

He seemed impressed. "That was pretty good."

"It wasn't 'pretty good.' It was awesome."

"I wish I had a bone."

"Never get into a legal argument with the Head of Ranch Security."

"Tomorrow's Christmas."

"I take no pleasure in crushing you in these debates. You must develop your skills."

"Maybe she'll give us some turkey bones."

"An educated dog should be able to...what did you say?"

He blinked his eyes. "When?"

"Just now, and will you hurry up? I have a ranch to run."

He rolled his eyes around. "Let me think here. Oh yeah, I said that I'll have to bone up on my debating skills."

"You said that?"

"I think that's what I said."

I gave him a pat on the shoulder. "Drover, I can't tell you how proud it makes me to hear you say that."

"How come you can't tell me?"

"I am telling you, or I was until you butted in."

"Oh, sorry. Tell me again."

"Very well, and please pay attention." I looked off into the distance. "You know, I don't remember exactly what I was saying. Maybe you could give me a hint."

"I think it was something about...turkey bones."

"I was talking about turkey bones?"

"I think so."

"Hmmm." I began pacing, as I often do when I'm trying to pull difficult concepts out of the vapors. "Turkeys have many bones, Drover, and the amazing thing is that they all fit together. If the bones didn't fit together and work in harmony, turkeys wouldn't be able to walk."

"Yeah, or play the drums."

"Drums?"

"Yeah, every turkey has two drumsticks."

"That's an interesting point. I've heard them cluck and chatter, but I can't say that I've ever heard them drumming."

"Maybe they do it in the middle of the night,

when we're asleep."

"I doubt that, son. I seldom sleep through the night. If I'm not out doing patrols, I'm at my desk, trying to catch up on paperwork. When you're Head of Ranch Security, the work never ends."

He yawned. "Yeah, and maybe we ought to go back to bed."

I stopped pacing and studied the runt. "You know, that's not a bad idea. If we dogs don't protect ourselves against stress and over-work, who will?" I marched back to my gunny sack, scratched it up, did the Three Turns maneuver, and flopped down. "We'll regroup at oh-eleven hundred hours. Good night."

"Nighty night."

I stretched out my weary body and surrendered myself to the powerful gravitational pull of my gunny sack bed. I lay there for two minutes, then sat up. "Drover, my bed smells so bad, I can't sleep. How about you?"

"Murgle skiffer porkchop."

"I agree." I leaped out of bed. "I've had enough of this. By George, if the people on this ranch are too cheap to buy new bedding for the Security Division, maybe it's time for us to take matters into our own hands."

"Furry little turnip tops."

"Unless we rise up in anger, the conditions around here will never improve. Stand by for action, son, we're fixing to tear this place apart!"

Boy, you should have been there to see it. We had ourselves a riot on the ranch, and we're talking about some serious ripping and tearing of the bedding. Once the terrible anger had begun to flow, it became a raging river and there was no force on earth that could have stopped it.

Birds quit singing. Rabbits ran for cover. Cattle and horses broke and ran in a wild stampede. Turkeys huddled in their roosting trees and turned their eyes away from the billows of black smoke rising from the ruins of the Security Division's Vast Office Complex.

It went on for days...or maybe hours. Okay, it went on for ten minutes, until the terrible rage had finally burned itself out. Callous neglect had pushed us over the edge of the brink and we had by George ripped up our stinking beds into piles of rags.

I was panting for air and standing over the ruins of my gunny sack bed, when I heard a voice behind me.

It said, "What are you doing?"

Slowly, I turned my head and saw...Drover.

He was staring at the rubble that had once been my bed. "We rioted against injustice and neglect and intolerable conditions, but I thought..." His gunny sack appeared to be undamaged. "You didn't riot?"

"No, I guess I was asleep, but I wondered what all the noise was about."

"It was about empowering dogs, Drover, and I can't believe you slept through such an historic event. This ranch will never be the same again."

"Yeah, 'cause now you're going to be sleeping on a pile of rags."

"That was the whole point. It was a protest."

"Yeah, but who was listening?"

That question hung in the air for a long, throbbing moment. When nobody answered, I walked back to my former bed and began sifting through the rubble, a hundred and twenty-seven shreds of burlap and a bunch of loose threads. I scraped them into a pile and sat down on them. They were lumpy and I could feel the cold ground beneath them, and they still stunk. Stank.

"Drover, it's possible that I acted in haste. Or, to come at it from a slightly different angle, you shouldn't have allowed me to do this."

"I was asleep."

"Exactly, and that's my whole point. At the

very moment when I needed you most, you abandoned me, but I'll try to forget about it."

"Thanks."

"Once we swap beds."

"Forget that."

"It's really the only decent course of action."

"Nope."

"I might even throw in a bone to sweeten the deal."

"No thanks."

"And one day's Scrap Rights."

"Nope."

"All right, then we'll have to *share* your bed."

"I'd rather not."

I was trembling with righteous anger. "You mean you'd actually allow the Head of Ranch Security to sleep on rags? Is that the kind of friend you've turned out to be?"

He thought about that and grinned. "Yep."

For a moment, I was speechless. "Then keep your stinking bed and see if I care. I have plenty of friends, and they would be honored to share their beds with me."

"That's nice."

"Traitor!" I whirled around and stormed out of the office.

CHAPTER TWO

Thinking About Food

One of the most discouraging parts of this job is that, after you spend years trying to set a good example for the employees, you find that they're just as selfish and greedy as they were before.

My assistant, Drover C. Dog, had become the most recent example of this slide into something-or-otherness. The nerve of the little pipsqueak! First he sat there and watched while I destroyed my bed, then he refused to share his possessions with the victim of a disaster.

I know I shouldn't let these things upset me, but they do. When you care about your employees, and I mean really care, it hurts when they let you down. Sometimes I'm tempted to lower my standards and accept that the world is a rotten place, full of selfish dogs and people, but I've never been able to pull that off.

Like a fool, I continue to hope, and it brings a lot of sadness into my life. Oh well. A guy must trudge on to the next chapter of his life, nursing the slender flame of hope.

Actually, that conversation with Drover had yielded a few shreds of good information. Perhaps you missed them, so let me give a quick review.

First, he had blurted out the fact that tomorrow, our people would observe the Christmas holiday. Second, he had pointed out one of the crucial differences between Christmas and every other day of the year: an evening Scrap Event that always produced an abundance of turkey bones and turkey skin, as well as occasional offerings of mashed potatoes, turkey dressing, turkey gravy, and even a few random bites of punkin pie.

Slurp. Sorry. The memory of past Christmas Scrap Events caused the slobbalary glands in my mouth to gush water, forcing me to lick my chops and make slurping sounds.

Slurp. See what I mean? It's funny how that works. A guy doesn't even have to see or smell the turkey-related material. Just the thought brings forth...slurp slop glop...it's a little distracting, to be honest, because a Head of Ranch Security must keep a clear, sharp mind at all times, and that's hard to do when he's having to mop his mouth every few slurps...every few seconds, shall we say.

Maybe we'd better change the subject. Where were we? I have no idea. Once you get those food thoughts inside your mind, it's hard to maintain a professional...tell you what, let's restart the story and see if that helps. Ready? Here we go.

It's me again, Hank the Cowdog. The mystery began in December, as I recall, and all I can think about are turkey scraps.

Okay, we're going to have to call a five-minute time-out and shut down all our equipment. Once we power up, please don't say anything about you-know-what. Got it? See you on the other side.

Equipment Is Shutting Down
Blank Screen
Blank Screen Sequence Is Still In Effect
This Is Boring
Equipment Is Ready For Power-up
Click, Whir, Buzz
We Have Power-up
Reconfiguring The Configuration

Waiting...Waiting
New Screen Is Loading
TURKEY SCRAPS!!!!!!!!

Oh brother. We know who's behind this: our enemies. They never rest or sleep. They're always on the prowl, searching for ways of hacking into our systems and planting bogus information that will breed chaos in the Security Division.

Who are they? We're never sure: cunning spies, robot monsters, creatures from the Black Latrine, strange beings from another galaxy, raccoons, coyotes, and cats. All we know for sure is that they're always slipping around and lurking in shadows, and we can never relax our scraps... relax our *guard*, that is. We can never relax our...

This is frustrating, but we have to mush on with the story. Getting bogged down in food thoughts is not an option. We'll just have to grit our teeth and try to crash through all the distractions.

Okay, after carrying on a depressing conversation with Drover in our office/bedroom, during which he had served as a willing accomplice in the destruction of my bed, I rode the elevator down to the first floor and walked out of the Security Division's Vast Office Complex.

The air outside was crisp and clean, and it helped clear my mind of all the fog that had accumulated during my conversation with Drover. All at once, it was clear to me that he was a selfish little cad, too stingy to share his bed with a fellow-dog, and that he needed to spend more time with his nose in the corner.

But the impointant pork is that it was a new day and I was determined to make it a good one. I marched past the garden with its bare stalks of last summer's okra, past the fragrant green waters of Emerald Pond (frozen, by the way), and up to the machine shed. There, I went straight to the overturned Ford hubcap that served as our dog bowl, and began crunching tasteless pellets of Co-op dog food.

Crunch, crack, snap.

I've already expressed my opinions about Co-op, so I won't take the time to repeat the obvious, that a first-class ranch outfit would have been embarrassed to put out such miserable fodder for its Security Division. It's bad stuff. I can't think of a nicer way of saying it.

So why was I eating it? Because a hard-working dog can't live on air, and also because eating Co-op served as a kind of vaccination against...well, temptation. You probably think that by the time a dog rises to the rank of Head of Ranch Security, he's beyond the reach of the kinds of temptations that torment ordinary dogs. Nice thought, but I'm sorry to report that it isn't true. I live with it day and night, and if you'll swear an Oath of Secrecy, I'll reveal the most dangerous form of temptation in the whole world—even more dangerous than turkey scraps.

Come closer so I can whisper this, and don't forget that you've taken a Solemn Oath of Secrecy.

Chickens.

There it is, and don't you dare spread this around. See, when a dog works around **CENSORED** every day of his life, it's best if he's not in a crazed condition and thinking about food. What we've found is that if he chokes down a few gulps of Co-op, it will soften his savage instincts and allow him to maintain a professional attitude about the **CENSORED**.

I'm sure you can imagine how important this is in the Overall Management Stragedy of the Ranch. Crucial. Extremely important. I mean, you wouldn't hire a bank robber to guard the vault of a bank, right? Well, it's the same deal on a ranch, because if the dog...

16

That's probably all we should say about this. You know how I feel about the little children. I wouldn't want them to think...enough said.

The point is that eating Co-op dog food wasn't a form of entertainment, but rather a standard procedure in our Overall Management Strategy. We endure a few moments of mild displeasure to avoid weeks of extreme discomfort with the Lady of the House.

Hencely, after experiencing a spell of Food Seizures, I thought it best to douse the fires of temptation, shall we say, and get on with my life, which included a routine walk around of ranch headquarters. It's something I do every day, even holidays—of which, by the way, the Security Division has none of which of which.

We get no holidays, no days off.

I walked through the corrals, stuck my head into the feed shed, checked out the saddle shed, the machine shed, and the chicken house.

Slurp.

Excuse me, and I hope you'll disregard that, uh, little outburst. It meant nothing, almost nothing at all. No kidding.

It took me two hours to do the Walk Around. A lot of dogs would have rushed through it and finished up in half an hour, but you know me. I'm pretty particular about these things and can't relax until I know that all is well on my ranch.

At that point, I noticed that a car was coming down the county road from the west. Near the mailbox, it slowed and made a right turn onto the road that led to the house. I narrowed my eyes and activated our Traffic Sensing Devices.

Was it the mail truck, the UPS man, one of the neighbors? We ran those options through Data Control's main system and got a negative. That left open the possibility that it might be some kind of unmanned probe that had been launched by The Other Side—our enemies, in other words.

Don't laugh. It happens. They're clever beyond our wildest dreams and just when you think, "They'd never do something like that," they do it. Unwary dogs get sandbagged every day, and some of them lose their jobs.

I hadn't planned on working Traffic, but this needed to be checked out. I switched on Sirens and Lights and went ripping around the north side of the house, just in time to intercept the unidentified vehicle as it approached the house.

You'll never guess who was inside the vehicle. You'll be shocked.

CHAPTER THREE

The Welcome Home Protocol

Ha ha. Okay, it was Sally May. No big deal. I guess she'd gone to town early that morning to buy groceries for the holidays. She was expecting kinfolks, don't you see, and they go through groceries pretty fast.

I switched off Sirens and Lights, went straight into Escort Formation, and led her to a secure parking spot behind the house. When she stepped out of the car, I was there to greet her with our Welcome Home Protocol.

Have we discussed the WHP? Probably not because it's kind of complicated, but very, very important. Do we have time to review the WHP? Sure, why not. Stand by.

Sally May Welcome Home Protocol #3543

1. Soft barks, low whines, broad swings on the tail, big smile with some teeth showing. The key here is moderation.
2. Show feeling and concern but maintain some distance. A few Leaps of Joy are okay.
3. Set barking levels at "Low." She doesn't like noise.
4. Don't jump on her.
5. Don't lick her on the ankles. She hates that.
6. Absolutely NO NOSE PRINTS on her clothing. Dark fabric shows every point of contact, and she'll think it's snot, even if it's good, honest nose water. One careless nose print can blow the whole program.
7. Don't get tangled up in her feet when she's carrying groceries to the house. She doesn't enjoy looking like an awkward cow, so try to respect her feelings on this.
8. Leave her cat alone. Beating him up is always fun, but you lose points.

End of SM-WHP #3543
File Will Now Self-destruct

So there you are. Pretty impressive, huh? You bet. Most of your ordinary mutts never give a thought to any of this, I mean, it goes completely over their heads. Me? I do whatever it takes to make the deal work.

Hencely, when she stepped out of the car, I went straight into Leaps of Joy, Wags of Delight, and just enough barking to let her know that, by George, we were sure glad to have her back on the ranch.

You'll be proud to know that I resisted the temptation to lubricate her car tires. That's normal procedure when we're working Traffic, especially when the driver is a cowboy, but over the years, we've learned that Sally May is...how can I say this without sounding harsh?

Over the years, we've learned that Sally May doesn't appreciate dogs rushing to her car tires and giving them a few squirts of Lubricating Emulsion. In fact, sometimes it really makes her mad. It's a puzzle and nobody in the Security Division has figured it out.

I mean, servicing tires is part of our job. We're glad to do it and don't even charge for it, but... well, if it makes her mad enough to screech at us, what's the point? We've found that everyone is happier when we leave her tires alone.

But I'll tell you something. It creates a bookkeeping nightmare. We have to keep a separate set of Service Records on all the vehicles. For Slim and Loper, we apply the Full Service Package, which means at least two squirts on each of the four pickup tires. If they're pulling a stock trailer, it doubles, eight tires.

But when Sally May's the driver, we have to switch to the Minimum Service No Warranty Package. It gets a little confusing sometimes.

So there she was, our Beloved Ranch Wife, back from her shopping expedition in Twitchell. When she stepped out of the car, I studied her face to get a reading on her mood. Your better breeds of cowdog are pretty good at this, don't you see, whereas your yip-yips and your low-bred mutts stand around thinking of new ways to say, "Duhhhh." Drover is the champion at saying, "Duhhhh." He doesn't read faces at all.

Me, I'm pretty good at it, and over the years, I've developed a kind of sick sense at gauging her mood. *Sixth* sense, it should be, not sick sense. See, we dogs have five basic senses: hearing, seeing, smelling, and I don't remember the other two, but the important thing to remember is that five senses make a nickel.

A little humor there. Ha ha. Did you get it?

Five senses make a nickel. Senses, cents. Ha ha. Around here, you have to pay attention or you'll miss a lot of good stuff.

Anyway, I'm pretty good at the so-forth, and my reading of her face told me that she was a little tired from the long trip into town (and riding herd on two children), but beyond that, she was in a happy frame of mind. It was my job to see that she stayed that way.

There she stood, outside the car, wearing a long black coat to protect herself against the north wind. My next reading of her face gave me a jolt. Steam was coming out of her nostrils, which is usually a sign of volcanic activity, and for a moment my finger edged toward the Escape button.

But then I figured it out. The air was so cold, her breath was making steam, and it had nothing to do with volcanic activity. I breathed a sigh of relief (hey, my breath made steam too), and right away, I started getting positive feedbag. She saw me, quivering with devotion, and doing it in a highly disciplined manner. That brought a smile to her lips, and we're talking about the sun breaking through a dark, cloudy sky. Big smile.

"Well, hello, Hank. Aren't we the polite gentleman today!" She offered her hand and I crept forward to receive Rubs and Pats. "Now, if I pet you, that doesn't mean I want to get pawed and trampled."

Oh, no ma'am. We'd studied the Protocol and this was going to be dignified and subdued.

I received the Rubs and Pats, and they were great. Hey, Sally May and I had gone through some dark times in our relationship, but this was the beginning of a new ear. A new *era*, I guess it should be, the beginning of a new *era*.

Would you like to guess who was lurking in the iris patch and watching with hateful, greedy eyes? The main clue here is "iris patch." Pete. Mister Precious. Mister Kitty Moocher. Mister Can't Stand To See Anyone Else Get A Pat From Sally May.

Yes, he'd been watching the whole thing from his loafing spot in the iris patch, and my huge success with the Welcome Home Protocol was eating his liver, big-time.

Here he came—not slinking or rubbing the paint off the side of the house, as he usually did, but coming with leaps and bounds. This was a cat on a mission—to ignite a bomb that would destroy my new relationship with Sally May.

I knew what the little creep had in mind, because he'd done it so many times before. He was just a dumb little ranch cat, but he had a streak of genius when it came to getting me in trouble with Sally May.

As he approached, wearing that insolent smirk that drives me nuts, I heard the sounds of a battleship coming to life: the blare of the claxon; the whir of gun turrets swinging around and leveling down at the target; the crisp click of the breech as high explosive shells slid into place.

"Captain, all weapons are loaded and ready to fire! Awaiting your orders, sir."

I held my breath as the cat came sliding into range—purring, grinning, fluttering his eyes. The pressure built inside my head and I heard a voice on the radio: "Captain, the target is acquired. Captain, do you copy? Captain?"

The tension had become almost unbuggable. Would I give the order to launch the weapon, surrender myself to the savage delight of thrashing the little snipe and running him up the nearest tree, and risk losing all my Goodie Points with the Lady of the House?

You probably think the answer is "yes," and at another time and another place, you might have been right. Sometimes I have the will power to back away from these hair-raising situations and sometimes I don't.

This time...I did.

I let the air hiss out of my lungs and gave the order to "stand down." That's a term we use in Security Work, "stand down." I don't know where it came from or why we use it. In certain respects, it doesn't make a whole lot of sense. I mean, you either stand UP or sit DOWN, and it seems a little absurd to order the men to "stand down."

Oh well. In the long view of history, it doesn't matter, but that's the kind of thing that activates a curious mind. Most dogs wouldn't give it a second thought.

Now, where were we? Oh yes, we had come to the brink of the edge and I had ordered the men to stand up and be counted, because we had an unauthorized cat coming straight toward us— smirking and purring and using all his kitty tricks that were clackulated to start a fire in the basement of my mind.

This was where it really got tough. I had to stand there and play Mister Doggie Perfect, while the cat rubbed on my front legs and flicked his tail across my nose. Oh, and whilst he was doing all of that, he also grinned up at me and said, in his most irritating whine of a voice, he said, "Well, well, it's Hankie the Wonderdog!"

My lips quivered. My jaws tightened. My

eyes burned holes in the little creep...but somehow I managed to snuff out the fires that were raging inside my mind. Instead of launching a full-scale invasion, I swallowed the bitter taste in my mouth, forced a counterfeit smile upon my lips, and said, "Hey, Pete, how's it going, pal, great to see you again."

His gaze lingered on me and his smirk slipped a notch. "Somehow I find that hard to believe, Hankie."

"No, it's true, Pete. Really. Honest. No kidding. Why, I was just thinking to myself...*get that tail out of my*...ha ha, I was just wondering how you'd been getting along."

"I've been getting along fine, Hankie, but even better now that Sally May's back on the ranch." He leaned forward and whispered, "She loves me, you know."

"Yes, I've noticed."

A dark shadow slipped across his face. "And it really annoys me to see her making a big fuss over a dog."

"Yeah? Well, get used to it, pal, because..." I caught myself just in the nickering of time. "Ha ha. I'm sure we can find a way to share her attention, Pete. It's a big world and everyone has a place in it."

His left eyebrow sprang upward. "You think so? I'm not so sure about that, Hankie. Right now, the world seems a little..." He gave me a wink. "...crowded."

And with that, he went slithering away, dragging his tail across my nose, and started rubbing on Sally May's ankles.

Fellers, you talk about Iron Discipline! I almost choked.

Sally May wasn't paying any attention to the drama that was unfolding at her feet. She told Little Alfred to start carrying bags of groceries into the house, while she walked around to the right side of the car to retrieve Baby Molly.

Guess who went with her, and I mean like her shadow, like flies on a piece of watermelon. Kitty, purring and yowling and trying to rub the hide off her ankles. It almost made me sick.

But you know what? It was starting to get on Sally May's nerves too. "Pete, honey, please don't get under my feet. I'd feel terrible if I stepped on you, okay?"

Do you suppose he took the hint? Ha! Of course not. Cats don't take hints. After they've figured out how to become a nuisance, they redouble their efforts and become even nuisancer.

As Sally May rounded the back of the car, it

finally happened. Old Pete, who was so adept at slithering through feet and ankles, made a slight miscalculation and got stepped on.

"REEEEEEEEERRRR!"

Sally May stumbled, trying to avoid smashing the little snot, and almost fell to the ground. She was horrified and, naturally, blamed herself. "Oh Pete, sweetie, I'm so sorry!"

She reached down to give him a pat and to ease his so-called pain, and would you like to guess what he did?

HE SCRATCHED HER!!!

Pete Gets In Trouble, Tee Hee!

For a moment, and we're talking about a long, throbbing moment, Our Beloved Ranch Wife couldn't believe what had happened. She stared at the cat, her eyes filled with hurt and shock, while the villain gave her a sultry, pouting glare. But as the seconds passed, the truth began to soak through the coffee filter of her mind.

She had just been clawed by her own precious kitty.

When I heard the whistle of air rushing into her lungs and saw the flash of lightning in her eyes, I had a feeling that kitty was fixing to get some schooling on whom to scratch and whom never to scratch.

He did. She snatched him up by his tail.

"Don't you ever scratch me again, you ungrateful little heathen!" Then she gave him a toss.

I was stunned. Astamished. Amazed. Never in my wildest dreams had I thought that I would live to see the day when she would call her cat exactly what he was, an ungrateful little heathen! And then give him a toss!

If I'd been in her shoes, I would have air-mailed him all the way back to the iris patch. She didn't throw him that far, but she got her point across. And don't forget that dogs don't wear shoes, so I could never have "been in her shoes."

Oh, this was wonderful! I rushed around the back of the car and began pumping out Barks of Applause.

"Hank, be quiet!"

Huh? I was just...hey, she was the one who'd tossed him. I was just...

Little Alfred, a normal, wholesome child, had reacted just as I had. He thought it was the funniest thing he'd ever seen, and he was laughing his head off. Sally May whirled around to him and gave him the Cobra Eye.

"And you, mister, don't you ever tell anyone about this!" A look of despair came to her eyes and she shook her head. "I can't believe I did that! I'm turning into a hag! Poor Pete!"

Poor Pete? Oh brother! What a waste of...

She hurried into the yard and tried to call the cat. "Kitty kitty? Pete, I'm sorry I lost my temper. I'm trying to get ready for company and...Pete?"

Do you suppose the ungrateful wretch came out of the bushes and tried to make peace with the woman who, for some weird reason, cared about him? Oh no. He saw this as a perfect opportunity to sulk and feel sorry for himself.

Sally May bit her lip and shook her head and returned to the car. "If he just wouldn't trip me... the poor thing!"

Oh brother.

She opened the car door and lifted Molly out of her seat. The baby had slept through the whole thing, missing the best show we'd had in years. Sally May told Alfred to start bringing in the groceries. "I'll put the baby down and be right back to help. And don't you dare be mean to the cat." She went into the house.

When Alfred heard the door close behind his mom, he felt free to release a big grin. "Boy, that was funny!"

Right, I thought it was hilarious, but it would have to be one of those secrets that dogs and little boys share in private. We had a special bond, don't you know, and it was built on a firm foundation:

neither one of us had any use for a cat.

Alfred fetched a bag of groceries out of the back of the car and started for the house. It was pretty heavy and he had to struggle to carry it. By the time he made it to the porch, he had to stop and rest. Setting the bag on the porch, he looked toward the house.

"Mom? It's too heavy. Mom?" He turned back to me and shrugged. "She's talking on the telephone."

Oh. Well, those things happen.

The boy glanced around, suddenly bored, and spied his toy bulldozer lying in the yard. He went to it, dropped down on his hands and knees, and started pushing it across the frozen grass. Moments later, the air was filled with the sputtering sounds of a D6 dozer, building a new road through the yard.

I heard a voice behind me. "Boy, that kid sure makes a lot of noise."

I whirled around and saw...Drover. "Traitor! Don't speak to me."

"Gosh, what did I do?"

"We've already discussed it. You're a greedy bedbug and I have nothing more to say to you."

"There's a cat in the car."

I had turned my back on him and resolved

never to speak to him again, but his statement—made very casually, I might add—caught my attention. I whirled around to him. "What did you say?"

"When?"

"Drover, don't start that again. My nerves aren't prepared to put up with your lunatic habits. Repeat what you just said and be quick about it."

"Well, let me think here. Oh yeah, I said there's a cat in the car."

I stared at him. "Pete's in the car?"

"Yeah, someone left the back door open and I think he's eating the groceries."

My eyes bulged against their sprockets. "He's eating groceries? Drover, why wasn't I informed of this?"

"Well, I just got here."

"Never mind." I pushed him out of the way and stormed over to the car. Sure enough, someone had left the back door open (we needn't name names, but you and I know who did it), and sure enough, there was a cat inside one of the sacks of groceries.

It was Pete, and would you like to guess what he was doing? With his switchblade claws, he had ripped a hole in a plastic bag and he was in the process of eating Sally May's bread!

The little crook. My entire body was swept by a wave of righteous anger. "Okay, Pete, Special Crimes is here. You're under arrest, pal. Hands up, get out of the car. Move!"

"Go away, Hankie. She hurt my feelings and I'm going to get my revenge."

"Revenge! Why you pampered little ingrate, get out of the car!"

He ignored me and kept right on eating. Oh, and you know how cats sometimes yowl when they eat? That's what he was doing, yowling and stuffing his face with bread.

"Pete, I'll count to three. If you're still there, we're coming in with guns blazing. One. Two!"

Drover rushed up beside me, grinning like a...I don't know what. "Git 'im, Hankie, git 'im!"

"Three!" The cat was still slobbering and gobbling. "Okay, that's it, you're toast. Drover, storm the car. I'll coordinate the operation from here."

His eyes grew as wide as plates. "Me! What about you?"

"We can't risk sending the Head of Security into a mission like this. It could be suicide."

"Oh. Well, no problem."

"That's the spirit!"

You probably think he jumped inside the car

and took care of business. Ha. He staggered three steps to the side and collapsed, and we're talking about falling like a bad load of hay.

"Drover, on your feet!"

"Drat the luck, this old leg just quit me. Help! Oh, my leg!"

"There could be a promotion in this."

"Oh, the pain! Oh, the guilt!"

My mind was tumbling. We had lost half our troops. The moans of the wounded filled my ears. What to do? Then it hit me, and we're talking about a stroke of genius. Instead of making a frontal assault, we would bark the alarm, alerting Sally May to the fact that her little crook of a cat was stealing bread.

Let *her* deal with the cat. I had a feeling that when she caught him in the act, her response wouldn't be, "Poor kitty!"

Was this a great idea or what? It was perfect, brilliant. See, this kind of thing had never happened before, kitty daring to rob groceries from innocent women and children, and doing it in daily broadlight. For years, he had managed to fool the general public and had keep his true, corrupt nature a secret.

Now he had given me a perfect opportunity to blow his cover and show the world what a rotten little creep he really was.

Sally May needed to know the truth about her cat, and she needed to be the one to drop the hammer on him.

Hee hee. I could hardly wait.

In making a dash to the house, I figured I would have to climb over Drover's prostrate body, only it wasn't there. Someone had moved it or… the little slacker! While I was occupied with other matters, he had highballed it to the machine shed.

"Double traitor! You will be court-martialed for this!"

Oh well, I didn't have time to deal with Drover. I sprinted through the yard gate (Alfred had left it open, of course) and rushed to the porch. There, I went into the Barking Stance (all four legs securely braced on a solid surface), loaded my lungs with a huge supply of carbon diego, and launched a barrage of Alert and Alarm Barking.

"May we have your attention please! The Special Crimes Unit has discovered a robbery in progress. Citizens of the ranch should arm themselves with brooms and fly swatters, and proceed to Sally May's car at once. This is a Code Three Emergency! Repeat: this is not a drill!"

Oh, you should have been there to hear it.

We're talking about thunderous barks, barks that rattled windows and shook the house to its very foundations. There was no way she could ignore such an amazing display of barking.

Sure enough, the door opened and her face appeared on the other side of the screen door. She looked mad. Good. She was fixing to be a whole lot madder—at her thieving little kitty.

The screen door flew open. BAM. I'm sure she didn't intend for the screen to crash into my nose, but it did. Water filled my eyes and for a moment, I thought I might sneeze, but we didn't have time for...

ACHOOO!

...sneezing.

ACHOO!

This was ridiculous.

In a voice that seemed a little stressed, she said, "Will you be quiet! I'm trying to talk on the phone to my mother-in-law, and I can't hear a word for all your noise."

Noise! Hey, even as we spoke, her cat was in the back seat...

"Hush!"

SLAM.

Oh brother.

CHAPTER FIVE

Portions of This Chapter Have Been Deleted

Well, what's a dog to say? We try to do our jobs. We stay up late, after everyone else has gone to bed. We do patrols, make reports, work in weather that isn't fit for man nor beets. We monitor the activities of crinimals and spies and postal employees. We study the clues and build our cases, and what do we get?

They tell us to hush, and slam the door in our face. In many ways, this is a lousy job.

You know what I should have done? I should have quit, resigned my commission, pitched them my badge and walked off the job. That's what ninety-nine percent of the dogs in this world would have done.

But you know me. Cowdogs have to be just a

little bit special. When the others quit and go to the house, we're still out there, protecting the ranch. It doesn't make sense and I can't explain it. That's just the way we're made.

So I guess you've already figured it out. I wasn't ready to quit the case. Too much was at steak...uh, at stake, we should say. Above all, I had to consider my relationship with Sally May. Lately, things had gotten better between us, and you might recall that upon her return from town, she had noticed my restrained, gentlemanly behavior.

That was a very positive sign and you can't imagine how long it had taken us to reach this point in our bonding process, after years of misunderstandings and faulty communication so-forths. Things were better now, and I just couldn't throw it all away.

But this case was complex because it involved HER SCHEMING LITTLE CAT. Everyone on the ranch seemed to think that he was Mister Kitty Perfect, that he never did anything wrong or even had a naughty thought.

Oh yeah? Well, this incident in the car was fixing to blow that theory right out of the water. I had the goods on kitty and, this time, no amount of treachery and lies could get him off the hook. I had Pete exactly where he wanted me.

Heh heh.

I loosened up the enormous muscles in my shoulders, lifted my head to the angle of maximum sternness, and began a fateful march toward the car. This time, there would be no Drover to chicken out, and there would be no fair warnings for the cat. We had worked up a simple Tactical Response: wade in, take no prisoners, and accept whatever wounds and casualties were required to clean out the thieves. Kitty might land a few lucky punches, but in the end, brute force would win the day.

At the open door of our Beloved Ranch Wife's car, I paused long enough to take one last snapshot of the crime scene. Kitty was so absorbed in vandalizing the family's bread supply, he didn't notice me. Good.

The Weapon was armed and ready. Three, two, one! Bonzai!

ROOF! ROOF!

"Reeeeeeer! Sssssssst!!"

Beautiful. Kitty never saw me coming, had no idea what hit him. He went off like a sack full of mousetraps, jumped straight up, hit the ceiling, bounced off a window, and—best of all—vanished without a trace, and we're talking about a blind

retreat out the car door.

Hey, we'd gone into this mission expecting to lose some skin or a piece of ear, but kitty was so shocked, he didn't land a single punch. I mean, we had cleaned his clock.

Okay, one punch, and it was the weirdest thing you ever saw. One of his stupid claws sank so deep into my upper lip that he couldn't get it out, and for several tense moments, we were, well, sort of welded together.

I showed him a mouthful of fangs. "Divv me my wip bap, you wittle kweep!"

"Well, give me my claw back!"

"I'll divv you your kwaw bap when you divv me my wip!"

"Hankie, I can't do anything until we disengage my claw. We'll have to call a fifteen-second truce."

"Otay, twuce."

I told you this was weird. For fifteen seconds, we stopped the war and worked together on getting his claw unhooked from my lip. At last, we got it out and I did what any normal, healthy American dog would have done. I gave him our Train Horns Barking Application, right in the face.

BWONK!

Hee hee. You should have seen him! He

turned wrong-side out, bounced off the ceiling, and went flying out the door.

"And let that be a lesson to you, for stealing bread from women and children!" Boy, you talk about a victory for the righteous! My whole body was tingling with the kind of righteous fury that comes to us when we...

Sniff sniff. What was that? Bread, but also something else.

Sniff sniff. Very interesting smell. Hmmmmm.

You know, once we've secured a crime scene and cleaned out the bad guys, the next step in the investigation is to, uh, go over the entire area with a fine-combed tooth, which means that we run our various sensing instruments over the...

That smell wasn't coming from the bread bag. It was some kind of meat.

Anyway, we laid out a grid and activated Snifforadar and began the tedious process of walking the instrument back and forth across the...WOW!

I froze in my tracks and moved my gaze from side to side. A water main exploded in my mouth, and all at once, I felt this powerful force that was...

This Section Has Been DELETED To Protect The Little Children

Anyway, nothing much happened. It was just a normal, routine wrap-up of a normal, routine crime scene investigation. We collected evidence, made some notes, dusted for footprints, the usual stuff.

You know, a lot of people and dogs think that Security Work is glamorous and exciting, but the truth is that it's just like any other job, mostly routine. Lots of reports and paperwork. Sometimes it gets a little boring, so we needn't go over every little turkey. Every little *detail*, let us say.

It was pretty muchly an open and shut case, in other words. We'd caught the cat in the act of robbing bread in the back of Sally May's car. For evidence, we had the plundered bread bag and cat tracks all over the scene, and all that remained was for Turkey May to haul the little thief into court and give him three swats with her broom.

Sally May, that is.

I would have loved to be there to watch the cat receive the thrashing he so richly deserved, but I, uh, had another appointment and needed to move along. I dived out of the...that is, I stepped out of the car and raced...I walked up the hill to the machine shed at a leisurely pace, whistling a little tune and, you know, enjoying the crisp cold air.

As I approached the machine shed, it occurred to me that Drover had fled to this very place (remember?) and that, well, he might need some counseling. He has a lot of problems, don't you see, and...well, if a guy ever gets too busy to help out a friend, he's just too turkey.

Too *busy*. He's too busy.

So I, uh, slipped through the crack between the big sliding doors and went inside. It was dark in there, but I knew where to find him. He's such a funny little guy, afraid of everything, and when he wants to escape Life Itself, he crawls into the darkest, backest part of the machine shed.

Sure enough, I found him in his usual spot, his Secret Sanctuary, sitting like a little statue made of stone. "Hey, Drover, how's it going, pal?"

"What are you doing in here?"

"Me? Oh, nothing, really, nothing much. I was just, you know, passing by and thought I'd check on you, is all."

I sat down beside him. There was a moment of silence. "What did you do this time?"

"I don't know what you're talking about."

"You never come in here unless you're in trouble."

"Drover, I'm really disappointed to hear you say that. Just because we've done certain things in the past doesn't mean...actually, we do have a small problem."

"Who's 'we'?"

"We, the staff and management of the Security Division."

"What happened?"

"Well, it's complicated."

"I'm getting out of here!"

"Drover, wait, come back! Drover?"

He sprinted to the door and dived outside, leaving me all alone with my, uh, problem. You're probably curious to know about my problem, but I'm not going to tell you.

Sorry, I can't. You know how I am about the little children. There are certain parts of my work that we just can't reveal to them, and that's all I can say.

CHAPTER SIX

Who Did It?

See, I'd gotten myself in kind of a mess. Something happened in the back of Sally May's car, but it's so dark and spooky, I can't talk about it. In other words, we have a story with a big hole cut out of the center. If we tried to mush on, nothing would make sense, but if we filled in the blank spot...

Oh, I know what you're thinking. "Go ahead, tell the truth, let it all hang out." It's not that simple. Listen, we're not talking about some little slip-up or a tiny lapse in judgment. This is...this is really dark stuff.

If I revealed the truth, little children all over the world would be crushed. They wouldn't be able to sleep. They'd stop eating their vegetables.

They'd forget to change their socks. And most of all, they'd think that I was a...

I can't do it, sorry.

So there I was in Drover's Secret Sanctuary and our story is stuck on high-center.

Anyone know a good joke?

Wait, here's an idea. What if we played the transcript of a conversation that would, uh, explain a few things? I don't have to admit anything, see, and you can listen to it and make your own judgment about whether it's true or just a pack of lies.

This might work. Okay, stand by to roll tape.

Transcript #373: Sally May and Alfred

Sally May: "Alfred, I thought I told you to bring in the groceries."

Alfred: "Well, I started to, but the sack was heavy."

Sally May: "All right, we'll do it together. Come on, and leave the bulldozer."

Alfred: "But Mom..."

Sally May: "Leave the bulldozer."

[Footsteps moving toward the car].

Sally May: "Your grandma is on her way with the boys and...Honey, you left the car door open. You shouldn't do that."

Alfred: "Sorry, Mom."

Sally May: "We have animals out here and..."

[Pause].

Sally May: "What happened to the bread?"

Alfred: "I don't know."

Sally May: "Something got into my bread. I need that for the turkey dressing."

Alfred: "It wasn't me."

Sally May: "Sweetie, that's why we must close the car doors. Our animals..."

[Pause. Long pause, really creepy.]

Sally May: "The *turkey*!"

Alfred: "What?"

Sally May: "Something got in here and ATE THE TURKEY! Look at this!"

Alfred: "Wowee."

Sally May: "Where is that dog? Hank!"

Alfred: "Mom, maybe it was Pete."

Sally May: "It wasn't Pete. I know exactly who did it, and if I ever get my hands on him...*I've got eight people coming for Christmas dinner!* Oh, this is going to be a complete disaster! IDIOT!"

Stop Tape
End of Transcript #373

Well, there it is, the missing piece of the story. Now maybe you understand why I was reluctant to, uh, release it to the public. Those were some serious charges that Sally May flang in my direction. Very serious charges. And now you have to weigh the evidence and decide the big question.

WHO DID IT?

Before you reach a verdict, allow me to review the case. First off, Sally May wasted no time in naming a suspect. Perhaps you noticed that she didn't study the evidence. She didn't measure the tooth impressions on the turkey carcass or make plaster molds. She didn't weigh the carcass or calculate the amount of meat that had been consumed.

Nor did she track down the cat to determine if maybe he'd gained five pounds in about fifteen minutes. Nor did she pay the slightest attention to the pleadings of her son—her very own flesh and blood, a fine, intelligent, morally upright young man who, upon seeing the plundered turkey, had made the only sensible statement to come out of the whole mess: *"Mom, maybe it was Pete."*

Nor did she interrogate any witnesses. Okay, there weren't any witnesses, but she might have at least asked my opinion. Don't forget, I was the first one to arrive on the crime scene. I would have been glad to give my testimony, but did she ask? Oh no.

She leaped to the conclusion that it couldn't possibly have been the work of her rotten little cat, and without looking at one shred of evidence, she screeched, *"It wasn't Pete. I know exactly who did it, and if I ever get my hands on him..."*

Ladies and gentlemen of the jury, it's not my job to sway your opinion to one side or the other. Okay, maybe it is my job, but I'm also trying to act as a mature, neutral third-party in this case, an objective voice of reason who, most of all, wants to see that justice is done.

What we have here is a rush to judgment. Sally May is a wonderful woman, but sometimes, in stressful moments, she leaps to wild, irrational conclusions that are based, not on evidence or hard facts, but on...well, on past behavior, unfortunate incidents that have haunted our relationship.

I won't try to whitewash my record. I'll tell you, up front, that mistakes had been made, but let me remind you that I've become an older dog, a wiser dog. And you can't convict a dog on past mistakes.

In conclusion, let me remind you who I am: the Head of Ranch Security. For years, I've battled enemy spies and monsters in the night, protected ranch property while everyone else was asleep, guarded the children, and barked wild animals away from her slurp chickens.

Would the Head of the ranch's Security Division eat his people's Christmas turkey in the back seat of a car, and then lie about it?

Thank you for your time. With that, I'll rest my case.

So what do you think? Before you answer, I have one more brief statement to make.

I did it.

There it is, out in the open. I can't let this thing drag on and on and turn into a twisted web of lies. **I DID IT!** Something happened to me in the back seat of the car. I turned into a maniac. I lost my mind. I ate the stupid turkey, and what I didn't eat, I wanted to eat.

It breaks my heart to admit this. It shatters my confidence. I've disappointed thousands of little children. I'm ruined. This is shaping up to be the worst Christmas of my entire life.

And of course, the greatest mystery of all is, why would a dog make such a bonehead mistake— eat a turkey that didn't belong to him, in broad daylight, when every human being within a hundred miles would NAME HIM AS THE PRIME SUSPECT?

Sally May rushed to judgment, but, unfortunately, she was right. Cats don't eat whole turkeys, and Drover was too much of a chicken to eat a turkey. So who or whom did that leave as a suspect?

Oh brother. What can I say? On the other hand...

Yes, let's look at The Other Hand. Number one, Sally May never should have gotten herself involved in a long-winded telephone conversation and left her groceries unguarded.

Number two, Little Alfred shouldn't have left the car door open, and it was totally wrong for him to start playing bulldozers. If he'd done what he was told, this never would have happened.

Number three...this is a big one. THE CAT. Who went straight to the open car door and began looting the food supply? It wasn't me. Hey, I was just trying to stop the looting, and while performing my duties as Head of Ranch Security, I happened to notice...well, the unguarded turkey.

Number four, when the people on this ranch feed us dog food made of sawdust and stale grease, we notice things like unguarded turkeys.

Hencely, a thorough review of the evidence leads us to one final conclusion: *I ate the turkey but it wasn't my fault.*

Whew! Boy, I wasn't sure we could get that deal worked out, and it looked pretty gloomy there for a while, but I think we've managed to put everything into perspective. Do you feel better about it? I do, and I'm really glad we've had this opportunity to work through all the issues.

You know, when people and dogs stop rushing around, when they slow down and think about their lives, they realize that "issues" aren't really "problems." They're just issues, and remember the wise old saying: "Issues are like tissues. Blow your nose on 'em and throw 'em in the trash."

Actually, I made that one up myself. Ha ha. But you have to admit that it's pretty good. "Issues are like tissues." Did you notice that it rhymes? Awesome. Sometimes I'm amazed at the things that come out of my mouth.

And speaking of my mouth, it had already put in a day's work. I mean, you didn't see what was left of that turkey in the back seat, but I can tell you: not much. We're talking about eating skin, bones, dark meat, white meat, pullybone, legs, the whole nine yards of turkey. Best turkey I ever ate.

But I'll tell you something about turkeys. They're easier to digest when they're...bork...

cooked. I'm not sure how to explain the difference, but it might have something to do with the bones. Raw bones are...erk...harder to digest than cooked bones, and there's something about raw turkey skin that...orp...

Hang on a second, we've got a little problem here.

Ump. Ump. Ump.

Okay, where were we? Oh yes, turkeys. Here's a piece of advice. If you're going to poach a turkey, choose one that's cooked. Raw turkey is about the nastiest kind of garbage you can put into your system. It's not exactly poisonous, but it will turn your gizzard wrong-side out.

Well! We've worked through our issues and have arrived at a Lesson For the Day, a lesson that should be directed toward young dogs all over America. "Leave the raw turkeys alone, boys, and wait for the scraps. You'll be glad."

Now we have to get back to the story.

CHAPTER SEVEN

The Blind
Turkey Trap

Around noon, Slim and Loper returned from feeding cattle. I poked my head through the crack between the machine shed's big sliding doors and heard bits of a conversation between them and Sally May. My name came up. I listened closely, hoping to hear someone say, "Hank would never do that."

That's not what I heard. Sally May named me as the villain and suggested that the men might want to go turkey hunting after lunch. Loper said they had to feed cattle. Sally May asked if he wanted to eat tuna sandwiches for Christmas dinner. Loper said they would shoot a turkey.

After lunch, the men emerged from the house, carrying shotguns and wearing peculiar clothing.

61

I overheard one of them say that they were "cammoed up." Maybe it had something to do with hunting. I'm pretty sure it had nothing to do with fashion, because they looked silly, walking around dressed like bushes. They got into the pickup and drove away.

By that time, I had been holed up in the machine shed for an hour and a half, and I was about to die of boredom. But suddenly, a brilliant idea sprang into my mind. *Hey, I could help them hunt a turkey!*

Since I had played some part in the, uh, Turkey Crisis, I felt an obligation to help them find a replacement for Christmas dinner. Yes, by George, it was the right and decent thing to do.

A lot of your ordinary mutts wouldn't have bothered going out on a cold December afternoon, but you know me. If I can lend a hand and help my people, I'm glad to do it—especially when my reputation has fallen under the shadow of suspicion.

To be honest, I was a little surprised that the men hadn't thought to invite me. I mean, what's a hunting trip without a loyal dog? For centuries, dogs had gone out with their masters, sharing the joy of a successful hunt and the disappointment of one that flopped. Around campfires, dogs had listened to hunting stories and laughed at stale jokes and provided the companionship that is so important in these situations.

I had a pretty good idea why they didn't invite me—because I don't come from bird dog stock. As you may know, we have something in this world called bird dogs. They have bird-instincts and bird-training and bird-brains. Hunting birds is all they know and all they ever think about. We're not talking about slightly abnormal. They are abnormal like you can't believe.

Me? I'm a cowdog and proud to be one. As a pup, I was raised in a cardboard BEEF box, not one that held spinach or carrots. I'm not a bird dog, in other words, but that doesn't mean that I can't go out on a hunt now and then, and help my guys locate a flock of wild turkeys. You don't have to be a twisted-genius bird dog to find turkeys. Shucks, I had found one in the back seat of a…

Let's skip that. It isn't funny. Forget I said it, okay? Thanks.

The point is that we cowdogs take pride in our versatility. We can load full-grown bulls into a stock trailer, guard little children, work Traffic, do Special Crimes and all the other things a well-balanced ranch dog needs to do. And when Duty calls us to help our cowboy pals bag a Christmas turkey, we can do that too.

The pickup pulled away from headquarters and headed north toward the mailbox. I trotted along behind it for a while, thinking they might realize that they'd forgotten me and, you know, slam on the brakes and yell, "Come on, Hank, load up!"

They didn't, but that was okay. They had other things on their minds. I was mature enough not to get my feelings hurt.

They turned right on the county road and drove east. Hmm. This was going to be more of a challenge than I had supposed, but I'm no quitter. I had observed them on several previous hunting expeditions, so I had a pretty good idea where they were going. In the past, they had driven down the road about half a mile, left the parkup picked in the ditch...left the pickup parked in the ditch, let us say, walked several hundred yards to the south, and set up a Blind Turkey Trap in some bushes near the creek.

That's where I went, cutting across country and following the creek to the east.

A lot of your ordinary mutts would have wondered, "How come the turkeys are blind?" And, come to think of it, I wondered about that myself. My best guess was that after they've been walking around all day in the bright sunlight, their eyes...something. They developed poor vision. Or maybe it was because they ate bugs all the time. If you eat enough bugs, it'll mess up your eyes.

The point is that when you're hunting turkeys, you look for the ones with bad eyes. They're hard to pick out of a crowd because they don't wear glasses, so you really have to pay attention.

Anyway, I trotted east through the pasture. About half a mile east of headquarters, I stopped on a little hill to reconoodle the situation. Sure enough, the pickup was parked in the ditch, with nobody inside. Just as I figured.

I continued my journey to the east, only now I slowed my pace to a Stealthy Trot, which means that I was covering ground but also able to do the full package of Visual and Nosatory Scans with the instruments. Very important, those scans. Wild turkeys aren't as dumb as you might think. In fact, they're pretty clever. It's always best to see them before they see you.

At this point in the mission, I saw no turkeys but did succeed in locating my hunting partners. Just as I had predicted, they were crouched down in some wild plum bushes north of the creek. Dressed in their funny-looking "cammo" clothing, they blended into the background and were hard to see.

Hmm. Do suppose that was the reason they'd worn the cammo suits? Maybe so.

Anyway, for those of you who have never gone on a turkey hunt, let me run through the basic strategy behind it. The guys wear a type of hunting attire that might cause a nearsighted turkey to think they are a tree or a bush. It makes the hunters look pretty silly, but they don't care.

We call it "cammo gear," and you're probably wondering where we got the word "cammo" and what it means. I happen to know, but do we have time for a lesson on Word Origins? Sure, why not.

"Ammo" is short for "ammunition," right? So it follows from simple logic that "cammo" is short for "cammunition." Properly speaking, when hunters hunt, they dress in cammunition clothes and carry ammunition for their guns which, when fired, make a loud noise called "bammunition."

You get it now? Cammo, ammo, and bammo. I get a kick out of learning new words and figuring out where they came from. As I've said before, without words, we'd all be speechless.

Okay, now we can get back to the turkey hunt. Slim and Loper had dressed up in their cammunition clothes, which caused them to blend in with the bushes. This kind of hunting outpost is called a Blind Turkey Trap. The idea is to lure nearsighted turkeys close enough so that the hunters can shoot one and take him home for Christmas dinner.

Wow, isn't it amazing that a cowdog would know so much about this stuff? You bet. Don't tell me that you have to be a bird dog to hunt turkeys. Any dog who has climbed through the ranks and become Head of Ranch Security can figure out how to hunt turkeys.

Well, I had spotted the hunters but they hadn't spotted me, so I crept on silent paws toward their Blind Turkey Trap, approaching them from the north. They were facing south, don't you see, and had no idea that I was coming to help. As I drew nearer, I heard them talking in low voices.

Loper said, "Can you believe that noodle-brain jumped into the car and ate the turkey?"

"Sure I can believe it. That's what noodle-brains do."

"Boy, he knows how to send my wife up in flames. I do that once in a while myself, but Hank makes me look like Clark Gable."

"Loper, fifteen plastic surgeons couldn't make

you look like Clark Gable."

"You're one to talk. If they cut off half your nose, it would still be twice too big."

"I've got a beautiful nose, only it was made backwards. My nose runs and my feet smell."

Loper chuckled. "That's pretty good. I'm sure you stole the line from someone else."

"Nope, made it up myself just now. Reckon we ought try the turkey call again?"

"I guess we should, unless you want tuna fish sandwiches for Christmas dinner."

"Hey, look! Turkeys. Shhhh."

"Don't shush me. You're the one who's been yapping."

"Loper, try the call."

Anyway, that's what Slim and Loper were doing in their Blind Turkey Trap, talking about nothing very important. And did you notice that my name came up in the conversation? It did, though you might not have recognized it. I think I was the one they referred to as "noodle-brain."

You know, one of the toughest parts of this job is putting up with all the trash we have to take from the cowboys. Make one little mistake and they...

Cack, cack, cack, cuckle cluck.

Wait, hold everything. Did you hear that?

Maybe not, because you weren't there, but I heard it. *It was the clucking of a wild turkey!* No question about it, and he was close, couldn't have been more than a few feet from Slim and Loper.

Do you see the meaning of this? While those two jugheads had been flapping their jaws and flinging insults at ME, a blind turkey had come right up to their Blind Turkey Trap!

After listening to their insults, maybe I shouldn't have cared about the success of their hunt. Maybe I should have let them go right on and mess up the chance of bagging a Christmas turkey, but part of being a cowdog is that you *care* about your people, even when you've lost all reason to care.

By George, somebody had to take charge of this deal, and it appeared that it would have to be me. I squared my enormous shoulders, grabbed a big gulp of air, and went charging into the middle of the plum thicket, barking at the top of my lungs.

"Hey, great news, I'm here to help you bag a turkey!"

Boy, were they surprised. They had no idea I'd been behind them, watching the whole thing, and old Slim just about wrecked himself when I came crashing through the brush.

But here's the odd part. The turkey I'd expected to find right in front of their noses... well, he wasn't there, so to speak, but there were twelve gobblers about fifty feet away, and when they heard me...

Drover and I
Have a Talk

O ops. The turkeys, uh, flew away

Okay, maybe there were parts of the
hunting strategy that I didn't understand. See,
Slim and Loper weren't actually hunting *blind*
turkeys. They were hunkered down in a spot
they called a "turkey blind" and they had this
little device, a "turkey call," that reproduced the
sounds of a...

How was I supposed to know? Half the time,
those guys are making jokes and the other half of the
time, they don't make any sense. How can a dog...

Boy, you talk about an eerie silence. After the
rush of turkey wings had faded into the distance,
we had several moments of very heavy silence.
Slim's eyes sagged shut and he slapped his forehead

with the palm of his hand. Loper's gaze drifted skyward and his lips formed words I couldn't hear.

I wasn't sure I wanted to hear his words. This scene had taken on the appearance of a, uh, very awkward situation. It seemed a good time for me to go to Looks of Remorse and Slow Puzzled Wags on the tail section, and to beam them the message, "Did I do something wrong?"

At last, Loper found his voice. "I am not believing this. Tell me it's a dream."

"It ain't a dream."

"I was ready to fire. I couldn't have missed. One more second and I would have had Christmas dinner."

"Goodbye to the turkey, hello, tuna fish." After a moment of scowling, Slim managed a little grin. "Say, that sounds like the title of a song. Didn't George Strait record it a couple of years ago?"

"I have no idea."

"Well, if he didn't, he should have. Loper, I've got this thing in my head and I think I can sing it for you. You want to hear it?"

"I'd rather run naked through a snow storm."

"Well, too bad. You're going to hear it. This time tomorrow, I won't remember it."

Loper heaved a sigh, unloaded his shotgun, and laid it on the ground. "Let's get it over with."

And with that, Slim belted out this song. If

you ask me, it wasn't nearly as funny as he thought, but you can make your own judgment.

Goodbye To the Turkey, Hello Tuna Fish.

Twas the day before Christmas on a West Texas spread.
Two cowboy employees were eating some bread.
The cupboard was empty, their spirits were down,
'Cause shopping for groceries meant going to town.

These boys weren't concerned 'bout the ice
or the cold.
Like cowboys of legend, they were fearless
and bold.
But shopping for anything gave 'em a rash.
That's how come their dinner was usually hash.

The mood in the bunkhouse had got pretty grim.
The hash was all gone and the pickings were slim.
The only thing left in the house they could eat
Was one can of tuna fish, hardly a treat.

Then Loper leaped up and said, "Slim, get
your gun!
We'll shoot us a turkey and have us some fun.
We'll bake it or fry it or make us some stew.
A tuna fish sandwich for Christmas won't do."

They hiked to the creek until they did find
A thicket of bushes that served as a blind.
Their cammo was perfect, the colors of fall.
They crouched in the bushes and started to call.

At first there was nothing, no track or a sound.
No sign of a turkey could even be found.
But then, from the distance, a sound reached
their ears:
The gobble of turkeys, and soon they were near.

The boys shared a wink, their spirits were bright.
Their dinner was coming, a Christmas delight.
But then a dark figure sprang out from the fog.
Nobody remembered to tie up the dog.

Old Hank wrecked the hunt and scuttled the boat.
The cowboys considered cutting his throat.
They said sad farewell to their Christmas wish.
Goodbye to the turkey, hello tuna fish.

They said sad farewell to their Christmas wish.
Goodbye to the turkey, hello tuna fish.

By the time he'd finished the song, old Slim
was wearing a big grin and rubbing his hands

together. "Boy, that's a crackerjack of a song."

"I didn't think it was all that great."

"It's the best one I ever came up with."

"George Strait wouldn't touch it."

"Well, I don't care. I ought to send it to somebody in Nashville."

"It's too late to buy a turkey. The grocery store closed at noon." All at once, Loper's gaze swung around and stuck me, and I mean like a fork. "What say we eat the dog for Christmas?"

WHAT? *Eat the dog?*

I glanced around, wondering if he might have been referring to someone else. I saw no other dogs and that gave me a real bad feeling. Gulp. I began easing backward, then whirled around and pushed the throttle lever all the way up to Turbo Seven.

Hey, I didn't know if those guys were joking or not, but when hunters start talking about eating the dog, it's time to move along. I did, fellers, and we're talking about Rocket Dog. I burned a hole through the frosty air and didn't slow until I had touched down in front of the Security Division's Vast Office Complex.

There, I rode the elevator up to the twelfth floor, hurried into my office, and closed the door behind me. Only then was I able to relax.

Actually, I didn't relax until I had opened the door a crack and peeked out into the hallway, just to be sure that...well, that my friends hadn't followed me.

Hey, don't laugh. I know it sounds crazy, two cowboys eating their dog for Christmas dinner, but those guys can be pretty strange sometimes. Just when you think they're goofing off, they'll come up with some new twist and...I couldn't afford to take any chances, is the point.

I went to the window and looked down at the city below: tourist boats on the river, taxi cabs moving like little yellow bugs up Forty-Second Street, couples walking arm-in-arm to the theater, laughing and having a wonderful time.

I was lost in thought, when I heard a voice behind me. "Oh, hi. What are you doing here?"

I turned and saw my assistant, lying on his gunny sack bed. "What am I doing here? I'm contemplating the ruination of my career."

"Gosh, that doesn't sound good. What happened?" I gave him a brief review of my day's disasters, starting with the store-bought turkey in Sally May's car and ending with the debacle in the turkey blind.

Drover gave me his usual vapid stare. "You don't have much luck with turkeys, do you?"

"Apparently not, and you know what breaks my heart?"

"The cowboys wanted to eat you?"

"No, that was a joke. I'm pretty sure it was a joke. They wouldn't actually eat their own dog, would they?"

He shrugged. "It might depend on how hungry they were."

"It was a joke. What really rips me is that in both instances, I was just trying to help."

"That's a little hard to swallow."

"It was very hard to swallow. Have you ever tried to eat and digest an entire raw turkey?"

"I'm not that crazy."

"Let me tell you something about raw turkeys. They come up a lot faster than they go down."

"You tossed it, huh?"

"Every particle. It's lying on the floor of the machine shed, even as we speak."

"Would you mind if I ate it?"

I glared at him for a long moment. "What? You'd actually...Drover, that's disgusting!"

"Yeah, but it's usually better the second time."

"Hmm, good point." I paced a few steps away. "No, I'd rather you didn't eat it."

"How come?"

"Because I worry about your health. And

besides, I might need it later on. These problems have clouded my future. I might have to remain in exile for days or even weeks. A guy feels better when he has a stash of food. I'm sure you understand."

He rose from his bed and started to leave. "I'd better get out of here."

"Wait, don't leave."

"Somebody might see us and think we're friends."

I stepped in front of him and blocked his path. "Drover, you have no choice. We *are* friends, and friends share each others' heartaches."

"You want to share mine?"

"What? You have heartaches?"

"Yeah, I get all depressed 'cause I have a stub tail."

"You expect me to listen to you whine about your tail?"

"That's what sharing means."

I really didn't have time for this, but… "Okay, tell me about your tail."

He sat down and a sad look came to his eyes. "All my life, I've had this chopped-off tail. I see all the other dogs with long tails and sometimes…" He began to sniffle. "…sometimes I just…I think I look ridiculous!"

"Hmmm. I see what you mean. It's sad, isn't it?"

"Yeah. All I ever wanted was to be normal."

"And that hasn't worked out too well, has it?"

"No! How can I be normal with a stub tail?"

I gave him a pat on the shoulder. "I understand, son, and I'm glad we've had this time to share. I think we've made huge progress."

"We have?"

"Yes. You're not normal and you look ridiculous. The sooner you accept it, the sooner you'll still feel abnormal and look ridiculous."

He blinked his eyes and cocked his head to the side. "I never thought of it that way. You know, I feel better now."

"Great. Now, let's get back to *my* problems." I paced a few steps away and gazed up at the gray sky. "Drover, I'm ruined. My job is hanging by a thread. Sally May hates me and the cowboys are talking about eating me for Christmas dinner."

"Maybe you ought to stay away from turkeys."

"Please don't dwell on the obvious. Believe me, I've learned my lesson. I will never *ever* look twice at another...Drover, may I ask you a personal question?"

"Sure. My life's an open book."

I whirled around and faced him. "At this moment in time, after all we've shared and been through, are you feeling...hungry?"

"Yeah, I'm starved."

"So am I, and you know, sometimes a good meal will bring perspective into our lives, bring everything down to earth, you might say."

"Yeah, but I'm tired of Co-op dog food."

"I'm not talking about Co-op." I paced over to him. "I know where we can find some leftovers."

He flashed a silly grin. "You mean..."

"Yes. By George, if we can't solve the problems of the world, at least we can eat a good warm meal."

"Gosh, you reckon it's still warm?"

"Warm enough for a couple of ranch dogs. Come on, son. To the machine shed!"

And with that, we left our troubles lying on the office floor and turned our minds to something lying on the floor of the machine shed. I think it would be best if we said no more about it.

Football With
The Boys

You don't need to know every detail of what we do in our work. It wouldn't make either of us wiser or richer, so what would be the point? Let's just say that Drover and I found some scraps in the...we found some scraps in an undisclosed location, and we'll leave it at that.

If you have further questions, you can ask them at another time. Nobody will answer them, but feel free to ask. This is still America.

It was a good, hearty, nutritious meal, and it confirmed the truth of two statements Drover and I had made earlier in the afternoon. Mine: "Sometimes a good meal will bring perspective into our lives." Drover's: "It's usually better the second time."

Both turned out to be true. A guy might not want to have reruns for every meal, but every once in a while, it works out pretty well. And you can't imagine how much our attitudes improved after we'd had a quiet, unhurried sit-down dining experience. When we finished, we felt twice as perspective as we'd felt before.

See, at some point during the dining event, all my cares and worries just seemed to melt away. Gone were the stabs of guilt and remorse, and gone were the oppressive clouds of...something. By the end of the meal, I felt that I had grown as a dog, had become older, wiser, and more mature.

Hey, I needed something to restore my confidence and renew my spiritual so-forths. A steady drumbeat of scolding and criticism will take the spirit out of a dog. When they accuse us of terrible crimes and screech at us and chase us with brooms...I don't know, it does something to our self-esteamer. It makes us want to tuck our tail between our legs and slink off to a dark corner.

Oh, and don't forget that business about "maybe we should eat the dog." That's a big-time confidence-killer. No dog wants to hear that from his friends.

Anyway, this new surge of confidence came at

just the right time, because as we were finishing our meal, we heard a car pull into headquarters. Grandma (Loper's mother) had arrived for the holiday, and with her had come two of Little Alfred's cousins. Boys. And soon the peace and tranquittery of the ranch were shattered by the noise of three boys running and yelling and chasing a ball.

I swallowed my last bite of undisclosed material and turned to my assistant. "The kinfolks are here. Let's go play football with the boys."

"Oh goodie, football." He must have seen the look of surprise on my face. "Did I say something wrong?"

"No, just the opposite. I'm shocked that you're going to play. You've never been one to exert yourself."

"Thanks."

"You're welcome. Let's go."

We stepped out of the machine shed and trotted down to that flat area just south of the gas tanks, where Alfred and his two cousins, Kale and Cameron, were throwing the football around. They were bundled up in coats and caps and gloves, and most people would have thought it was too cold for football, but these lads didn't notice the weather.

They had visited the ranch a few times in the past and we'd had a grand old time playing together. As you may know, there's a special bond between boys and dogs, and if you ask me, it all traces back to one thing: boys are easy. They do normal things, such as chase balls, climb trees, build hideouts, make noise, and wrestle in the grass. Those are boy-things, but they're also dog-things, except climbing trees. We aren't so good at climbing trees.

See, when a dog hangs out with a gang of boys, he can feel...well, comfortable just being a dog. We can chase 'em around, jump on 'em, bark at 'em, bite their pant legs, trip 'em to the ground, roll around in their arms, lick 'em on the face, and run off with their gloves.

If we stink, they don't care. If we slobber on 'em, they wipe it off and go on. If we tear their clothes, they don't take it personally. If our play gets a little rough and they get banged up, well, who cares? They're just boys.

With little gals, it's a different deal. No decent ranch dog would take pleasure in cart-wheeling a girl, and if he did, he'd never say, "Oh well, she's just a girl." No sir. That would be rude, crude, uncouth, and socially unacceptable. They're special, those little gals, and a dog can do certain things with the gals that he could never do with the boys, such as...well, fall in love.

Remember Alfred's two girl cousins, Ashley and Amy? They came to the ranch one Thanksgiving and I thought I didn't like girls. Ha. Boy, did I get an education! Hey, after we'd played Tea Party and Dress Up and Beauty Shop, I'd fallen so deeply in love, I couldn't find the light switch or the front door. I mean, we're talking about head-over-heels, lost-at-sea-and-never-coming-back kind of love.

Yes sir, they're special, those little gals, and a dog needs to be on his best behavior. With boys, you never fall in love, but everything is easy. All you have to do is be a dog.

So I was really looking forward to spending time with those boys—three boys and a dog on a ranch in the Texas Panhandle. Now, doesn't that sound like the beginning of a great adventure? You bet, and they were playing football, my favorite sport. They were even using a peewee-sized ball, the kind that a dog can hold in his mouth as he streaks down the sideline for a touchdown.

When Drover and I arrived on the scene, Alfred gave me a warm welcome, and right away, started telling his cousins the whole story about my unfortunate encounter with his mother's you-know-what. He'd also heard about The Turkey Hunt That Went South, and he told that one too.

To be honest, I was ready to put all of that behind me and get on with my life. But you know what? Kale and Cameron laughed their heads off. They thought it was the funniest thing they'd ever heard, and all at once, I became...well, a kind of celebrity. It was pretty neat.

See what I mean about boys? They're easy. They have a kind, forgiving nature. They understand temptation and naughty behavior, and they know that, just because a dog poaches a turkey now and then, or blows up a hunting adventure, it doesn't make him a Bad Dog.

It was a shame the adults on the ranch didn't take a lesson from the boys, but we can't dwell on that.

The impointant point is that we chose up sides and played a big game of pass and touch. The lads called it the "Turkey Bowl." I thought that was an unfortunate choice of titles, but nobody asked my opinion. The teams were: me and Kale against Alfred and Cameron.

You're probably wondering why Drover didn't get drafted. He did. He was supposed to play on Alfred's side, but he made such a mess of it,

Alfred kicked him off the team and sent him to the sidelines. He was supposed to play on the defensive line, see, and rush the passer. You know what he did? Every time the ball was hiked, he sat there and barked.

Oh brother. I was embarrassed. Naturally, getting thrown off the team broke his little heart, and he sniffled all the way to the sidelines, limping on his so-called "bad leg." But he got no sympathy from me or the boys. No sir. We'd been chosen to play in the famous Turkey Bowl, and we didn't have time to fuss over the slackers.

You might be surprised that I was the big star of the game. No kidding. And you're probably dying to hear how I did it. Well, I didn't plan on giving away my football secrets, but maybe it wouldn't hurt.

Okay, here's the deal. A dog will never make All-Pro as a quarterback or wide receiver, for the simple reason that we can't throw or catch a pass. So we have to make it at other positions. I've tried 'em all: defensive line, cornerbuck, laidbacker, goalie, shortstop, you name it. But I've found that my skill set (that's a technical word we use in sports business skill set) is best suited to running back.

I even have a few pointers for those young

dogs out there who are dreaming of making a career in football. Here's my list.

Show up in your best physical condition and keep your body in top shape. Nobody wants to hear about your "bad leg."

Learn the rules of the game and don't cheat unless it's absolutely necessary.

Try not to drool on the ball.

And finally (this is the big one), don't let the other guys touch the ball, hee hee. The first time one of the guys on the other team drops a pass, snatch up the ball and start running. It doesn't matter which way you run, just run around. They'll chase you and try to get the ball back, and sometimes it makes 'em mad, but a clever dog can figure out how to stay one step ahead of a bunch of boys, especially when it's cold and they're all bundled up in heavy clothes.

The main advantage of this technique is that it gives the dog a chance to show off his speed and moves, and to become the star. The main disadvantage is that...well, sometimes it kills the game.

Actually, that happens fairly often, so maybe we'd better add one last rule. Football is a team sport and if you don't give the other players a chance to do something, they'll eventually get tired

of chasing you around and go do something else.

And, well, that was more or less what happened at the Turkey Bowl. I turned in one of the most amazing performances of my whole career (fifteen touchdowns, three hundred yards rushing), but... well, they cancelled the game at the end of the first quarter.

The boys walked off the field, and said they were going down to the creek to build a fort or something. And you know what? They didn't invite me to go along. To tell you the truth, it kind of hurt my feelings.

So there I was, standing on the fifty yard line of this huge stadium and looking around at all the empty seats. All at once it seemed just a big lonesome place. I glanced around and saw Drover, still sitting on the sidelines, gazing off at the clouds and wearing his usual dreamy expression.

You know, when a guy has lost all his other friends, he develops an appreciation for Drover. In many ways, he's a weird little mutt, but steady. He's always around, and when you're down to your last friend, he can become your best friend in the whole world.

I drifted over to him and sat down.

CHAPTER TEN

A Boy In Trouble!

Drover didn't notice me, so I cleared my throat. At last his gaze floated down from the clouds. "Oh, hi. Tomorrow's Christmas."

"That's correct.

"It sure is cold."

"It's very cold."

He glanced around. "I thought you were playing football."

"I was, but the boys got in a huff about something and quit."

"I'll be derned. I wonder what happened."

"I have no idea."

A grin spread across his mouth. "Oh, I get it. You hogged the ball."

"How would you know that? You were staring

at the clouds."

"Yeah, but you always hog the ball and it always kills the game."

"Oh brother. I can't believe you'd make such slanderous remarks about a superior officer."

"Yeah, but it's true."

There was a moment of silence. "Okay, your remarks were slanderous and disrespectful, but I'm willing to admit that they might have contained a germ of truth."

He sneezed. "Uh oh, I thig you just gave be a jerb."

"I gave you what?"

"A jerb."

"I did not give you a germ. Don't forget, it was *your* slanderous remark that contained the germ of truth."

He sneezed again. "Well, subwud gave be a jerb."

"It wasn't me, so don't go around spreading lies—or germs. Sneeze in the other direction, would you?" A cold gust of wind blew a tumbleweed across the empty football field. "It's kind of lonely without the boys, isn't it?"

He sneezed again. "You're dever alode whid you've got hay fever."

"You'll have to explain that. It makes no

sense."

"Well, whid you sdeeze all the tibe, you don't deed toys or frids. You've always god a sdeeze to keep you compadee."

I stared into the vacuum of his eyes. This was a level of weirdness the world had never seen before, and it was clear that I needed to change the subject, before he went completely off into space.

"Let's talk about something else. Tomorrow is Christmas day."

"I already said thad."

"Please hush. Tomorrow is Christmas day and I was wondering if you'd come up with any gift ideas for...well, ME, for example?"

"Doe. You wad sub jerbs?"

"No, I don't want any germs. However," I laid a paw on his shoulder, "my gunny sack is in tatters and, well, this might be a good night to share a bed for Christmas. What do you think?"

"Doe thags."

"You don't have to decide this minute."

"Doe thags."

"Take your time, give it some thought."

"Doe thags."

I felt my eyes bulging. "Selfish goat!"

"Subwun just screebed."

"I can't believe you'd allow the Head of Ranch Security to…what did you say?"

"Subwun sceebed."

"Someone screamed?"

He pointed a paw toward the south. "Yeah, down ad the creeg. Baby it's the boys."

Just then, my ears leaped up to the Max Gathering Position. "Wait, hold everything. Someone just screamed down at the creek."

"Thads whad I said."

"Don't you get it? The boys went down to the creek!" I leaped to my feet. "You don't suppose… they wouldn't be playing on the ice, would they?"

All at once, he began limping around in circles. "Oh drad the lug, this old leg's giving be fids."

"Stand by, son, we've got a Code Three down at the creek! Ignite all engines and close canopies! Ready?"

"Oh, by leck!"

"Launch all dogs! To the creek!"

Boy, you talk about smoke and flames and a roar that rattled the trees! I blasted off and went streaking into the sky, setting a speed course that would take me directly to the creek. I leveled off at thirty thousand and glanced over both shoulders, looking for my wing man.

He wasn't there. Just for an instant, a chill of

fear crawled down my spinal backbone, but then I remembered Drover's last words: "Oh, by leck!" If you translate that out of Sinuseeze, it means, "Oh, my leg!"

So, once again, my assistant had...oh well, I didn't have time to fumigate about Drover and his leg problems. Something bad was happening down at the creek and I had to get there, double-quick.

When I arrived on the scenery, I knew we had a problem. Kale and Cameron stood on the north bank, looking toward the frozen creek. Right away, I did a head-count: one, two. We were short one boy. Alfred.

I rushed up to the boys. Their faces were as pale as sheets and their eyes wide with fear. "Hank the Cowdog, Search and Rescue. What's the problem?"

For a moment, they couldn't speak, then Kale pointed a mittened hand toward the creek. "Alfred fell through the ice!"

Right then, I heard a scream and saw Alfred's head bobbing above the water. My blood went cold, not only because it was cold out there, but mainly because my little pal was in serious danger...and I HAD NO IDEA WHAT TO DO!

For several moments, we had sheer chaos,

might as well go ahead and admit it. All three of us ran around in circles. Cameron and I ran into each other, knocking both of us to the ground.

But by the time I had leaped back to my feet, I knew what had to be done. When things are at their very worst and all else has failed, brave dogs rise to the occasion and BARK! Yes sir, I barked, the deepest, loudest barks I could come up with.

"Bring up those trucks! Extend that ladder! You there, throw him a line! Blankets, get blankets! Move, move, move!"

It was a very impressive display of barking, but...you know, sometimes barking helps and sometimes it just makes noise, and after several minutes, I realized that we were going to have to change the plan.

I rushed over to Kale, the older of the two boys, and tried to beam him an urgent message through tail-wags. "Son, I need your help. Do you hear me?"

He was so scared he couldn't talk. I licked him on the face and it seemed to help.

"Run to the house. Get help. Hurry. Do you understand?" He gave his head a nod. "Cameron and I will stay here and...I don't know what we'll do, but run for help!" Kale set sail for the house...

and Cameron went with him. "Hey, come back here! Don't leave me here alone! Wait!"

Too late. They were on their way to the house, yelling for help and running as fast as their little legs would carry them. And me? Gulp. I was alone with a little boy who was thrashing around in the icy water and crying out for someone to help him.

You know, sometimes when an emergency strikes and we're called upon to test our limits, we, uh, don't respond as well as we'd wish. Sometimes we do things that, later on, seem... well, kind of pointless. I'm not proud to report this, but we might as well be honest.

You know what I did to help my little pal? I started *chewing my paw!* I know, it sounds crazy, but there I was, all alone, scared out of my wits, helpless, useless, and all I could think to do was... oh brother, chew my paw.

Yes, that sounds crazy, but what did you expect me to do? Creep out on that sheet of ice and run the risk of getting dumped into the freezing water?

Forget that. Have we discussed ice water? Let's talk about it. I HATE ICE WATER! I hate being cold and wet in the wintertime. Hey, if Alfred wanted me to save him, he should have fallen into the creek in July. I would have been glad to dive in and give him some help.

But in the middle of December? There was no way this dog was going to…

"Hankie, help me! Help me, please!"

His voice was getting weaker, a tiny cry in a frozen world.

I took a deep breath and squared my enormous…no, my shoulders weren't enormous. They were thin, weak, and pitiful, and they felt like spaghetti. I was beyond scared, but you know what? All at once my mind was clear.

This wasn't going to be fun.

I crept out on the ice. "I'm coming, son, don't worry about a thing." My paws slipped and slid on the ice. "Remember the time in the summer when we came down here to fish? Boy, we got in trouble with your ma! She was so mad, she wanted to skin us alive."

The ice snapped and cracked beneath my paws. "It was hotter than blazes, remember? Think about how hot we were that day and keep your head out of the water. Good job, nice work. I'm almost there."

I made it to the hole in the ice and looked down into his face. His skin had a bluish tint and there was a look of desperation in his eyes, as though he knew…I extended my right foot. "Here, pal, grab hold and I'll see if we can pull you out."

He grabbed my paw with a hand that was weak and frigid. I pulled back with all my strength and tried to dig my claws into the ice. I felt myself slipping toward the water.

"Listen, buddy, let's try something else. If you keep pulling…"

He hung on and kept pulling. I couldn't stop… and slid into the water.

Words can't express the explosion of awful sensations that greeted me when I felt that ice water closing around me. It caused me to gasp, but after a bit, I caught my breath and gave my pal an easy smile.

"Hang on and hold me close. Maybe I can warm you up a little bit." He wrapped his arms around my body and I dug my front claws into the edge of the ice, enough to keep our heads out of the water. "Whatever happens, we'll be together."

After a while, I didn't notice the cold any more.

CHAPTER ELEVEN

We Are Frozen Solid

What makes you think there's more to this story? I mean, Alfred and I were in a very dangerous situation, floating around like a couple of polar bears in a frozen pond.

What if nobody came to our rescue? What if Cameron and Kale got lost and never made it to the house? What if Alfred and I turned into blocks of ice?

Sometimes those things happen, and every story doesn't have a happy ending, just because we want it to.

Fellers, things were looking bad. Alfred held me close and I hung onto the ice and we managed to keep our snoots out of the water until, after what seemed hours, we heard footsteps coming from the house.

My neck was so frozen, I could hardly turn my head, but I did anyway and saw Loper and Slim, my hunting buddies, coming at a run—the same guys who had talked about eating me for Christmas dinner.

That didn't exactly warm the cockleburs of my heart, but I noticed that Slim was packing a ten-foot wooden ladder and Loper had a catch rope in his hands. Sally May and the boys came right behind them, and Sally May had an armload of blankets.

When Alfred saw them, his pitiful little voice cried out, "Daddy! Mommie!"

The men didn't waste a second. Loper yelled, "Put the ladder on the ice, and be careful. The ice might not hold you." He thought about that. "No, I'll do it."

Slim pushed him away. "You've got a wife and kids to support."

Slim stepped off the creek bank and onto the ice. It began making cracking sounds. He set the ladder on the ice and slid it out, so that the far end reached to the pool where we were. He got down on his hands and knees and started crawling toward us on the ladder.

Would the ice support his weight? That's

what everyone was wondering as we held our breath and watched long cracks shooting across the surface of the ice.

Closer and closer he came, inch by inch. The ice popped and groaned under his weight, but he kept coming. "Alfred, hang on, I'm almost there." His eyes were fixed on the boy and his breath made fog in the air. At last, he stopped and reached out his hand. "Take my hand."

Alfred shook his head and moaned, "I'm so cold...help!"

Slim looked back at Loper. "Build a loop in that rope and pitch it here." In a rapid motion, Loper made a loop in the rope, swung it over his head, and floated it out to Slim. He caught the loop and turned to Alfred.

"Son, we need to get this rope under your arms and around your body. Can you do that?"

"I don't know, hurry!"

Slim moved out on the ladder as far as he dared. The edge of the ice began to break away, and for a moment, it appeared that the whole thing might collapse. But it didn't. Slim reached out his long arm and dropped the loop around Alfred's head and shoulders.

"Okay, slip it under your arms. There you go, good!" Slim zipped the loop tight around Alfred's

chest. He looked back at Loper and yelled, "We've got him, haul away!"

Loper turned against the rope and put every ounce of strength into the tug. Sally May dropped her blankets and joined him on the rope, and together they hauled one half-frozen little boy out of the water and up to dry land.

Kale and Cameron let out screams of joy and started jumping up and down. Sally May grabbed the blankets and rushed to Alfred, wrapped him up in wool and held him in a tight embrace. She picked him up and started back to the house, holding the precious bundle tight in her arms.

Well, it was a great moment for the people on our ranch, but in all the excitement, they had forgotten one small detail. ME. I was still in the water, and by that time, my body had grown so numb, I lost my grip on the edge of the ice. I tried to hang on but the old paws just quit working.

When my head slipped under the water, Slim was looking toward the north, a big smile on his face. He didn't notice me. I moved my paws and tried to dog-paddle to the surface, but it didn't help. I sank.

They say that at times like this, your whole life flashes before your eyes. You know what flashed before my eyes? That recycled turkey on the floor of the machine shed. In that last quiet moment, I found myself wondering, "Did I actually eat that stuff?" The answer was yes, and it had given me the most incredible indigestion you can imagine...not that it mattered any more.

And I guess that's about the end of the story, don't you suppose? I can't think of any way to keep it going. I mean, let's face the truth: dogs don't function well underwater, especially icy water on a cold December day.

So maybe we ought to just say our goodbyes and go our separate ways. It won't be the same without me around, but you'll be okay. Try to remember that I'd had a good life and that when it came to the end, Old Hank took care of his friends.

We've had a good run, but this case is...

[Keep reading, there's more]

Heh heh. Did you really think I was going to check out? It sure looked that way for a while, but I'm happy to report that it didn't get quite that far.

The first indication that my luck was fixing to turn came when I heard a muffled voice calling my name. "Hank? Hey, where'd you go?"

As you can imagine, I was glad that somebody had noticed me missing, so I tried to bark a reply. "Blub, blub, blubber!" Don't forget, I was underwear. Underwater, that is. I was underwater, and still sinking.

Did you happen to notice that those two words look almost the same, underwear and underwater? They look the same but they're not. I get a kick out of it...we'd better get back to business.

You're probably wondering what I was using for air. Not much, and that was becoming a problem. If I didn't come up with some air pretty quick...

Then something grabbed me by the ear. I was a little fuzzy in the head by then and figured I'd been grabbed by a lobster or something.

It kept pulling on my ear, and by George, the next thing I knew, my head popped out of the water and this...this giant lobster was crouched on a ladder on the ice and doing something with a rope.

Well, you know me. When giant lobsters start

pulling on my ears, I don't just sit there looking simple. I bark. "Blub!" It wasn't much of a bark, but it was the best I could come up with.

Then the lobster yelled, "Got 'im! Pull!"

And, what do you know, I went flying out of the water and got sledded across twenty feet of ice that was very slick and cold. When I hit dry land, I tried to sit up but...well, it appeared that I'd left my legs in the water. I couldn't move and now two gigantic lobsters were standing over me and...

Wait, hold everything. You thought I was about to be eaten by a pack of lobsters? Ha ha. Like I said, my head was a little foggy and....Loper and Slim. Ha ha. See, they'd fished me out of the water and...wow, they hadn't forgotten me after all.

I was actually alive and had all four legs attached!

Slim's right arm was wet all the way up to his shoulder, his shirt was turning to ice, and his teeth were clacking together. He said, "Let's head for the house before me and Hank die of the shivers."

Right. I was lying on the sandy bank, soaked to the bone and shaking from head to tail. Loper looked down at me. "Can you walk to the house?"

Walk? No. My legs were frozen stiff. I couldn't even stand, much less walk.

He grumbled, wrapped me up in a blanket, and hefted me off the ground. "Good grief, you weigh a ton!" He staggered a few steps, then we headed for the house, about two hundred yards to the north.

Slim pulled on his coat and walked beside us. He was cold and tired, but still had enough juice left to make a joke out of this deal. "You know why he's so heavy, don't you?"

"It has nothing to do with the size of his brain."

"No, you're packing a dog plus your Christmas

dinner. Heh. I know that makes you proud."

See what I mean? They never quit joking, those two. It doesn't matter how cold it is or how serious the situation. But old Slim got a little more than he bargained for. Loper was huffing and puffing by then. He stopped and tossed me into Slim's arms.

"If you've got enough energy to flap your mouth, carry the dog." He walked away, smiling. "Sure is a pretty day."

Slim carried me the rest of the way and did quite a bit of muttering, but it was mostly under his breath. When we reached the yard gate, guess who arrived on the scene. Mister Oh-My-Leg.

"Oh my gosh, what happened? Did I miss something?"

"You missed everything. I saved a drowning child and almost froze to death."

"Drat the luck! I hate it when this old leg quits me. But it's feeling a little better now, and so is my hay fever."

"Great. I hope you and your leg enjoy staying out in the cold, because I've got a feeling they're going to take me inside the house."

His jaw dropped. "No fooling?"

"That's right: warm house, soft bed, satin

sheets, the whole nine yards of royal treatment. No more stinking gunny sack for me, pal, and let this be a lesson to you. Slackers miss out on all the good stuff."

Sure enough, the men went through the gate and up the sidewalk toward the house. On the porch, things got even better. Sally May's pampered little sneak of a cat came flying out of the iris patch and scrambled up on the porch. As you might expect, the sight of me being carried into the house sent him into convulsions of jealousy, I mean, we're talking about a cat that had lost his mind and was trying to rub the boots off Slim's feet.

He didn't quite get that done, but he managed to snake himself around Slim's ankles and caused him to stumble. Good old Slim. He'd always had a special touch with the cats. He didn't get mad or yell. He just slipped his boot under kitty's belly and gave him a ride back to the iris patch.

Hee hee, ha ha, ho ho. I loved it!

We went into the house, leaving Drover standing at the gate, a look of tragedy etched on his face.

CHAPTER TWELVE

Joy To The World

Wow, what a deal! I had earned a free trip into a warm house on Christmas Eve!

You probably think they put me out in the utility room, with the washer and dryer, the mops and coats and muddy boots. No sir, they carried me into the very innersanctamum of the house, the living room with soft furniture, carpet on the floor, and a big, friendly, wood-burning stove.

Oh, and did I mention the Christmas tree? Yes sir, we had us a big juniper tree that Slim and Loper had found in one of the canyons. They had cut it and brought it to the house in the back of the pickup, and now it was decorated with all kinds of pretty stuff: lights and glass balls, little angels with harps, plastic birds, and strings of popcorn and cranberries.

Everybody was there: Grandma with baby Molly in her arms; Sally May, Loper and Slim, and my three teammates from the Turkey Bowl. Little Alfred sat next to the stove, wrapped up in a blanket and sipping hot soup. When they set me down beside him, the lad threw his arms around my neck.

"Hankie, you saved me and you're my friend forever!"

Would you believe that everyone clapped and cheered? They did, honest. And then Sally May said, "Let's take a moment to be thankful." She turned her eyes to Loper.

He closed his eyes and bowed his head. "Lord, we're so thankful for this home and for Alfred's safe return. We're even thankful for my wife's dog. He ate our turkey but saved our boy. In Thy holy name we pray, amen."

For a moment, nobody said a word. Eyes darted around the room and the boys were biting back their grins. Then Grandma let out a chuckle and soon everyone in the house was laughing. I was a little bewildered by it all as I glanced from face to face. I mean, obviously there had been a joke somewhere, but I didn't get it.

Oh well, it was a great day to be alive and

unfrozen, and a great day to be a dog. Sally May brought me a bowl of warm milk and watched, beaming a smile, while I lapped it down. When I had finished my milk and licked the bowl clean, she knelt down beside me and looked into my eyes.

"Hank, I'll swan, sometimes you make me so mad, I could pinch your head off."

We were getting off to a bad start.

"But you were there when it mattered. Thank you for what you did."

She pulled me into a hug and pressed her cheek against my burp. Excuse me. She pressed her cheek against my face, and what lousy timing.

She pulled away and stared at me for a long, throbbing moment, fanning the air in front of her face. "There, you see? I try to give you some love, and you *belch in my face!*"

Yes ma'am, but if you'd seen what I ate...you know, if you ask me, turkey is way overrated and I don't know why it's so popular at Christmas. But the impointant point is that you should never burp when you're being hugged by a lady. It really turns them off.

But the good news was that she was able to laugh about it and didn't throw me out into the cold. No sir, I stayed right there beside the stove and took part in the family's Christmas Eve festivities. Sally May made popcorn and hot chocolate, and the boys and I invented a new game called Shoot Baskets At The Dog.

You ever play it? Wonderful game, good wholesome entertainment. It was kind of like basketball, don't you see, only instead of shooting a ball, the boys used popcorn. Would you like to guess what they used as the basket? Heh. Me. And you might say that I ate it up.

You'll be proud to know that I didn't miss a shot. Okay, one bounced off the rim, but I got the rebound. Great game.

After supper, everyone gathered in the living room beside the tree and Loper read the Christmas story from the Bible, then they sang Christmas carols until bedtime. At that point, I began to worry about...well, my lodgings for the night. I mean, I had dried out and recovered my strength, but the thought of spending Christmas Eve night out in the cold, on a pile of stinking rags...

But then I noticed that Loper and Sally May had gone off to a corner and were whispering about something, and their eyes seemed to be darting in my direction. It made me uneasy, until I heard her say, "Oh, all right, just this once."

Whew! Did you get the meaning of that? She'd decided to let me spend the night in the utility room—in the house! It was a little drafty out there, but she dug around in the cedar chest and brought out a Hudson's Bay four-point wool blanket, and she let me use it for a bed!

What a deal, huh? You bet. For warmth, you can't beat those wool blankets.

They got me settled in my bed and were about to turn out the light, when Loper went to the back door and looked out. "Hon, poor little Drover's out there at the gate, shivering and looking pitiful. It's pretty cold. The thermometer says seven degrees. Maybe we could..."

Sally May scowled. "Oh, all right, but he doesn't get a wool blanket. He can sleep on a bath mat."

Moments later, Mister Shivers was curled up on his bath mat, beside me on the floor of the utility room. When Loper and Sally May went off to bed, he raised up and gave me his patented silly grin.

"It worked. I thought maybe it would."

"Congratulations. I hope you'll be on your best behavior. The Security Division doesn't need any more smudges on our record."

"Oh, you don't need to worry about me. I'm just glad to be out of the cold." His grin faded and he looked at my bed. "How come you get a wool blanket and I get an old bath mat?"

"Because I performed an act of heroism and you performed an act of chickenism."

"Yeah, but it doesn't seem fair."

"It's as fair as it needs to be, and as good as you deserve. Good night." I stretched out on my bed and began switching off the circuit breakers of my mind.

"How is it?"

"What?"

"How's your bed?"

"Drover, I never dreamed a bed could be so soft, comfortable, and warm. If you ever get a chance to sleep on a Hudson's Bay four-point blanket, you'll love it, but of course you never will."

"I don't reckon you'd share, would you?"

"No. Good night."

That's about the end of the...okay, there was one small incident that occurred in the night. You probably think that it had something to do with Turkey Reruns, but that wasn't it.

Or maybe you think that I tore up Sally May's favorite wool blanket. Yikes, that would have been awful and I don't even want to think about it. But that wasn't it either.

Along about three o'clock in the morning, Drover woke me up. He said he was freezing on

his little cotton bathmat, and begged to share my bed. He didn't deserve it, but I invited him into the warmth of my Hudson's Bay four-point wool blanket—and had to listen to him squeak and grunt through the rest of the night.

Oh well, it was Christmas.

And that's about all of the story. Wow, what a finish! I had become a hero, kept my job, humbled the cat, and spent the night in a warm house.

Oh, one last thing. Sally May wasn't kidding about the tuna fish. That's what they ate for Christmas dinner, tuna casserole, but the thing to remember is that it wasn't my fault. Little Alfred shouldn't have left the car door open, right?

Thanks, I knew you'd understand. We'll see you down the road.

This case is closed. And Merry Christmas.

Have you read all of Hank's adventures?

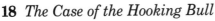

Join Hank the Cowdog's Security Force

Are you a big Hank the Cowdog fan? Then you'll want to join Hank's Security Force! Here is some of the neat stuff you will receive:

Welcome Package
- A Hank paperback
- An Original (19"x25") Hank Poster
- A Hank bookmark

Eight digital issues of *The Hank Times* with
- Lots of great games and puzzles
- Stories about Hank and his friends
- Special previews of future books
- Fun contests

More Security Force Benefits
- Special discounts on Hank books, audios, and more
- Special Members-Only section on website

Total value of the Welcome Package and *The Hank Times* is $23.99. However, your two-year membership is **only $7.99** plus $5.00 for shipping and handling.

☐ Yes I want to join Hank's Security Force. Enclosed is $12.99 ($7.99 + $5.00 for shipping and handling) for my **two-year membership**. [Make check payable to Maverick Books.]

Which book would you like to receive in your Welcome Package?   (#   ) any book except #50

_____

BOY or GIRL

YOUR NAME   (CIRCLE ONE)

_____

MAILING ADDRESS

_____

CITY   STATE   ZIP

_____

TELEPHONE   BIRTH DATE

_____

E-MAIL   (required for digital Hank Times)

Send check or money order for $12.99 to:

Hank's Security Force
Maverick Books
PO Box 549
Perryton, Texas 79070

DO NOT SEND CASH. NO CREDIT CARDS ACCEPTED.
Allow 2–3 weeks for delivery.
Offer is subject to change.

The following activities are samples from *The Hank Times*, the official newspaper of Hank's Security Force. Please do not write on these pages unless this is your book. Even then, why not just find a scrap of paper?

For more games and activities like these, as well as up-to-date news about upcoming Hank books, be sure to check out Hank's official website at **www.hankthecowdog.com**!

"Photogenic" Memory Quiz

We all know that Hank has a "photogenic" memory—being aware of your surroundings is an important quality for a Head of Ranch Security. Now you can test your powers of observation.

How good is your memory? Look at the illustration on page 91 and try to remember as many things about it as possible. Then turn back to this page and see how many questions you can answer.

1. Which was higher: Hank's Ears, Feet, or Tail?

2. How many buttons were on Alfred's coat? 1, 2, 3, or 4?

3. Was Hank looking to HIS Left or Right?

4. Hank had a ball: Base, Soccer, Foot, or Basket?

5. Were there more clouds on the Left or Right of Alfred in the picture?

6. How many of Alfred's feet could you see? 1, 2, or all 3?

"Rhyme Time"

What if Sally May decides to make a little extra money for a family vacation? What kind of jobs could she find?

Make a rhyme using SALLY MAY that would relate to her new job possibilities.

Example: SALLY MAY opens a tanning salon.

Answer: SALLY MAY RAY

1. Sally May starts a pottery business.

2. Sally May becomes a cheerleader and leads cheers.

3. Sally May starts a diet center to help people lose pounds.

4. Sally May teaches dogs to sit where they're told and not move.

5. Sally May becomes Santa's transportation chief.

6. Sally May invents a special board people can eat on while watching TV.

7. Sally May writes a story that actors perform on stage.

8. Sally May invents a machine that makes triangle shaped bales of this.

9. Sally May teaches people the proper way to respond to a question.

10. Sally May creates a new color shade of paint.

Answers:

1. Sally May CLAY
2. Sally May YEAH
3. Sally May WEIGH
4. Sally May STAY
5. Sally May SLEIGH
6. Sally May TRAY
7. Sally May PLAY
8. Sally May HAY
9. Sally May SAY
10. Sally May GREY

"Word Maker"

Try making up to twenty words from the letters in the name below. Use as many letters as possible, however, don't just add an "s" to a word you've already listed in order to have it count as another. Try to make up entirely new words for each line!

Then, count the total number of letters used in all of the words you made, and see how well you did using the Security Force Rankings below!

SALLY'S TURKEY

_____   _____

_____   _____

_____   _____

_____   _____

_____   _____

_____   _____

_____   _____

_____   _____

_____   _____

_____   _____

59-61   You spend too much time with J.T. Cluck and the chickens.

62-64   You are showing some real Security Force potential.

65-68   You have earned a spot on our ranch security team.

69+   Wow! You rank up there as a top-of-the-line cowdog.

John R. Erickson, a former cowboy, has written numerous books for both children and adults and is best known for his acclaimed *Hank the Cowdog* series. He lives and works on his ranch in Perryton, Texas, with his family.

Gerald L. Holmes has illustrated numerous cartoons and textbooks in addition to the *Hank the Cowdog* series. He lives in Perryton, Texas.